This is a duck.
A duck called Brian.

What's that you say?

He's blue?

He sure is.

He's a real one of a kind!

For the purposes of this story, it's important that you know that Brian's favourite things in the world are:

1. His best friend, Gregory

TO BRIAN,

YOUR FRIEND, GREGORY

2. A cold glass of milk

MILK

YUM

MILK FACTS

MOO!

A SPLASH O' THE GOOD STUFF

INGREDIENTS: MILK

DELICIOUS DUCK NUTS

YES!

HOW DA YA LIKE 'EM?

100%

NUTTY

3. A bowl of delicious Duck Nuts.

On the day of our story, things did NOT start well.
When he went to the cupboard for his morning
Duck Nuts and milk, Brian discovered he had none left.
This was a disaster.

He decided to go and find Gregory to tell him all about it.

Gregory was not at home and he was not at the pond.

I shall try the park,

TUM-TE-TUM

thought Brian.

On his way there, Brian came across Peter, who was busy counting ants. 'Good morning, Peter,' said Brian. 'Have you seen Gregory?'

Sorry, no... I've been busy counting ants. Would you like to join me?

'That does look like fun,' said Brian.
'But I need to find Gregory.' And he carried on his way.

Next, he came across Neil and Tina, who were icing a gigantic cake. 'Good morning, Neil and Tina,' said Brian. 'Have you seen Gregory?'

'That does look like fun,' said
Brian. 'But I need to find Gregory.'
And he carried on his way.

He came across some other ducks, some crocodiles, and an almost certainly crocodile-proof diving suit. 'Good morning,' said Brian. 'Has anybody seen Gregory?'

'That does look like fun,' said Brian.
'But I need to find Gregory.' And he carried on his way.

Next, he came across a near record-breaking pyramid of ducks. 'Good morning,' said Brian. 'Has anybody seen Gregory?'

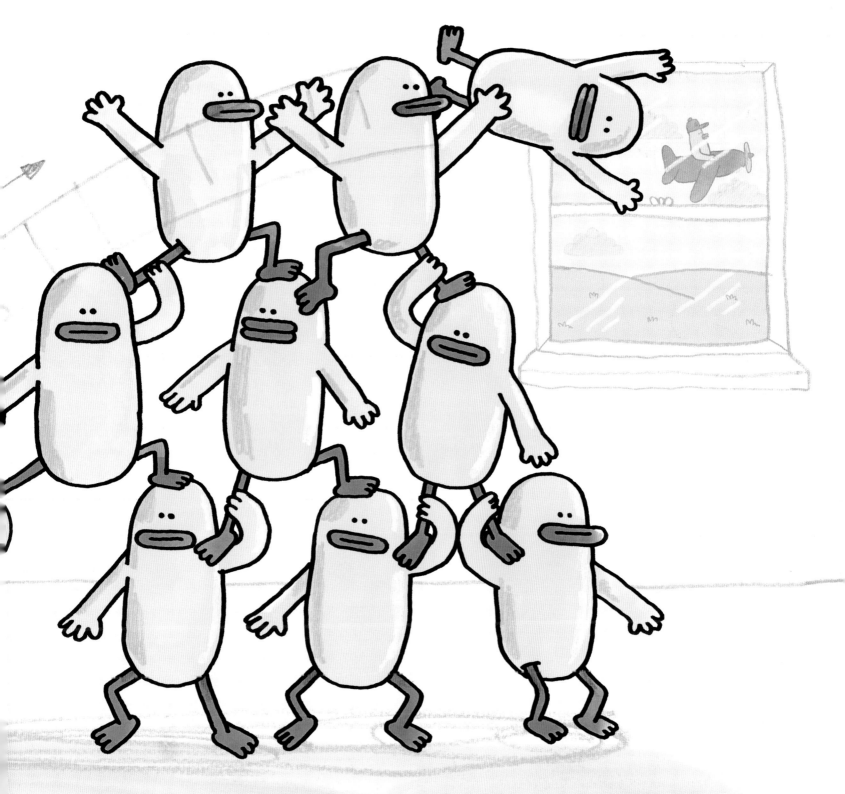

'That does look like fun,' said Brian.
'But I need to find Gregory.' And he carried on his way.

Soon, he came across some terrified ducks and a dangerously out-of-control Siberian snow leopard. 'Good morning,' said Brian. 'Has anybody seen Gregory?'

Sorry, no... We've been busy trying to tame our dangerously out-of-control Siberian snow leopard. Would you like to join us?

'That does look like fun,' said Brian.
'But I need to find Gregory.' And he carried on his way.

Later on, he came across a state-of-the-art space
rocket with Gareth strapped to the back.
'Good morning,' said Brian. 'Has anybody seen Gregory?'

Sorry, no...we've been busy building a
state-of-the-art rocket to send Gareth to
the moon. Would you like to join us?

'That does look like fun,' said Brian. 'But I need to find Gregory.' And he carried on his way.

Later still, Brian came across a group of sunbathing ducks in what appeared to be a mass sunbathing festival. 'Good morning,' said Brian. 'Has anybody seen Gregory?'

Sorry, no... we've been busy taking part in a mass sunbathing festival. Would you like to join us?

'That does look like fun,' said Brian.
'But I need to find Gregory.' And he carried on his way.

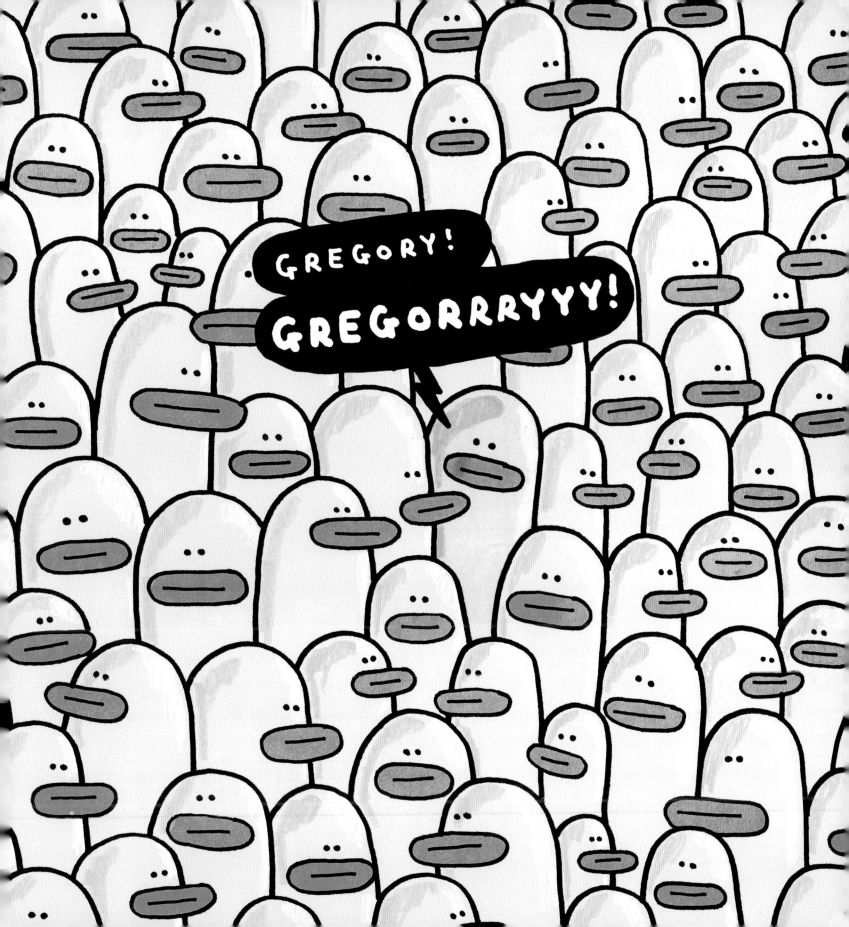

'This is the **worst day** EVER.
I'm out of Duck Nuts and milk,
and I can't find my best friend anywhere!'

Brian sat down with a huff.

Suddenly, Brian found himself floating through a magical land. There was a magic frog floating on a magical lily pad—classic magic door stuff.

You finally found us! We've been waiting all day for one lucky winner to find our magic kingdom AND HERE YOU ARE!

And can you guess what happened?

And with that, Brian's wish finally came true.

As the sun set, the two friends agreed that perhaps it hadn't been *quite* such a bad day after all.

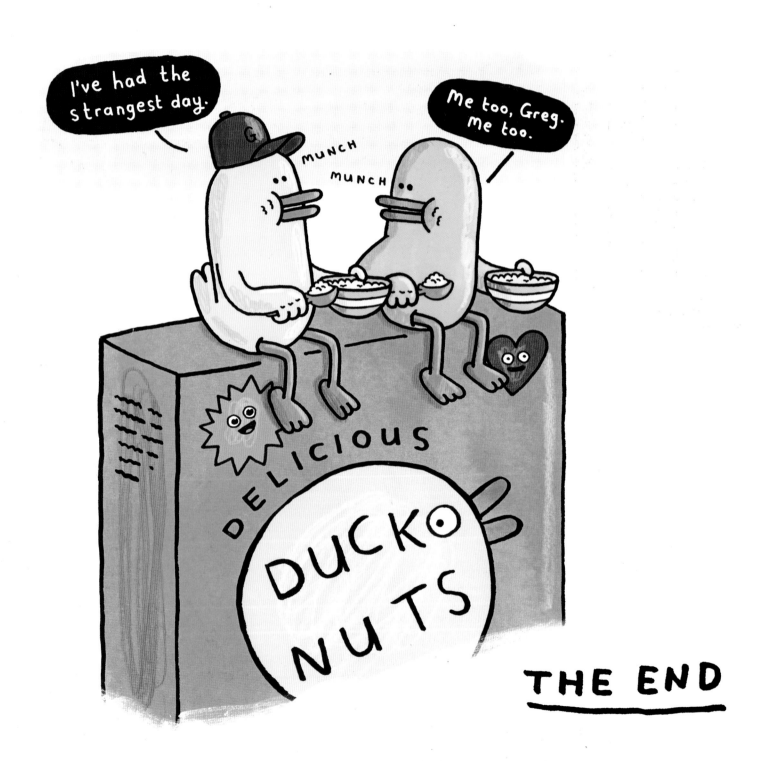

THE END